The Mystery of Marie Roget

By

Edgar Allan Poe

THE MYSTERY OF MARIE ROGET

A SEQUEL TO "THE MURDERS IN THE RUE MURGUE"

means to occur at the same time

There are ideal series of events which run parallel with the real ones. They rarely coincide. Men and circumstances generally modify the ideal train of events, so that it seems imperfect, and its consequences are equally imperfect. Thus with the Reformation; instead of Protestantism came Lutheranism.

—Novalis.Moral Ansichten.

There are few persons, even among the calmest thinkers, who have not occasionally been startled into a vague

means belief

idea of someone who is very smart.

yet thrilling half-credence in the supernatural, by coincidences of so seemingly marvelous a character that, as mere coincidences, the intellect has been unable to receive them. Such sentiments—for the half-credences of which I speak have never the full force of thought— such sentiments are seldom thoroughly stifled unless by reference to the doctrine of chance, or, as it is technically termed, the Calculus of Probabilities. Now this Calculus is, in its essence, purely mathematical; and thus we have the anomaly of the most rigidly exact in science applied to the shadow and spirituality of the most intangible in speculation.

The extraordinary details which I am now called upon to make public, will be found to form, as regards sequence of time, the primary branch of a series of scarcely intelligible coincidences, whose secondary or concluding branch will be recognized by all readers in the late murder of Mary Cecilia Rogers, at New York.

When in an article entitled "The Murders in the Rue Morgue." I endeavored, about a year ago, to depict some very remarkable features in the mental character of my friend, the Chevalier C. Auguste Dupin, it did not occur to me that I should ever resume the subject. This depicting of character constituted my design; and this design was thoroughly fulfilled in the wild train of circumstances brought to instance Dupin's idiosyncrasy. I might have adduced other examples, but I should have proven no more. Late events, however, in their surprising development, have startled me into some farther details, which will carry with them the air of extorted confession.

[handwritten margin note: a type of behavior that is unusual to norm]

Hearing what I have lately heard, it would be indeed strange should I remain silent in regard to what I both heard and saw so long ago.

Upon the winding up of the tragedy involved in the deaths of Madame L'Espanaye and her daughter, the Chevalier dismissed the affair at once from his attention, and relapsed into his old habits of moody reverie. Prone, at all times, to abstraction, I readily fell in with his humor; and, continuing to occupy our chambers in the Faubourg Saint Germain, we gave the Future to the winds, and slumbered tranquilly in the Present, weaving the dull world around us into dreams.

But these dreams were not altogether uninterrupted. It may readily be supposed that the part played by my friend, in the drama at the Rue Morgue,

starts to become ↑ reknown for the solving previous mystery

had not failed of its impression upon the fancies of the Parisian police. With its emissaries, the name of Dupin had grown into a household word. The simple character of those inductions by which he had disentangled the mystery never having been explained even to the Prefect, or to any other individual than myself, of course it is not surprising that the affair was regarded as little less than miraculous, or that the Chevalier's analytical abilities acquired for him the credit of intuition. His frankness would have led him to disabuse every inquirer of such prejudice; but his indolent humor forbade all farther agitation of a topic whose interest to himself had long ceased. It thus happened that he found himself the cynosure of the political eyes; and the cases were not few in which attempt was made to engage his services at the Prefecture. One of the most remarkable instances was that of

the murder of a young girl named Marie
Rogêt.

This event occurred about two years
after the atrocity in the Rue Morgue.
Marie, whose Christian and family name
will at once arrest attention from their
resemblance to those of the unfortunate
"cigar-girl," was the only daughter of the
widow Estelle Rogêt. The father had
died during the child's infancy, and from
the period of his death, until within
eighteen months before the
assassination which forms the subject of
our narrative, the mother and daughter
had dwelt together in the Rue Pavée
Saint Andrée; Madame there keeping a
pension, assisted by Marie. Affairs went
on thus until the latter had attained her
twenty-second year, when her great
beauty attracted the notice of a
perfumer, who occupied one of the
shops in the basement of the Palais

Father
(dead)

Estelle Rogêt
(mon)

Marie
(daughter)

Royal, and whose custom lay chiefly among the desperate adventurers infesting that neighborhood. Monsieur Le Blanc was not unaware of the advantages to be derived from the attendance of the fair Marie in his perfumery; and his liberal proposals were accepted eagerly by the girl, although with somewhat more of hesitation by Madame.

The anticipations of the shopkeeper were realized, and his rooms soon became notorious through the charms of the sprightly grisette. She had been in his employ about a year, when her admirers were thrown into confusion by her sudden disappearance from the shop. Monsieur Le Blanc was unable to account for her absence, and Madame Rogêt was distracted with anxiety and terror. The public papers immediately took up the theme, and the police were upon the point of making serious investigations, when, one fine morning, after the lapse of a week, Marie, in good health, but with a somewhat saddened air, made her re-appearance at her usual counter in the perfumery. All inquiry, except that of a private character, was of course immediately hushed. Monsieur Le Blanc professed total ignorance, as before. Marie, with Madame, replied to all questions, that the last week had been spent at the house of a relation in the country. Thus the affair died away, and was generally forgotten; for the girl, ostensibly to relieve herself from the impertinence of curiosity, soon bade a final adieu to the perfumer, and sought the shelter of her mother's residence in the Rue Pavée Saint Andrée.

It was about five months after this return home, that her friends were alarmed by her sudden disappearance for the second time. Three days elapsed, and nothing was heard of her. On the fourth her corpse was found floating in the Seine, near the shore which is opposite the Quartier of the Rue Saint Andrée, and at a point not very far distant from the secluded neighborhood of the Barrière du Roule.

The atrocity of this murder, (for it was at once evident that murder had been committed,) the youth and beauty of the victim, and, above all, her previous notoriety, conspired to produce intense excitement in the minds of the sensitive Parisians. I can call to mind no similar occurrence producing so general and so intense an effect. For several weeks, in the discussion of this one absorbing theme, even the momentous political topics of the day were forgotten. The Prefect made unusual exertions; and the powers of the whole Parisian police were, of course, tasked to the utmost extent.

Upon the first discovery of the corpse, it was not supposed that the murderer would be able to elude, for more than a very brief period, the inquisition which was immediately set on foot. It was not until the expiration of a week that it was deemed necessary to offer a reward; and even then this reward was limited to a thousand francs. In the mean time the investigation proceeded with vigor, if not always with judgment, and numerous individuals were examined to no purpose; while, owing to the continual absence of all clue to the mystery, the popular excitement greatly increased. At the end of the tenth day it was thought advisable to double the sum originally proposed; and, at length, the second week having elapsed without leading to any discoveries, and the

The reward is doubled

prejudice which always exists in Paris against the Police having given vent to itself in several serious émeutes, the Prefect took it upon himself to offer the sum of twenty thousand francs "for the conviction of the assassin," or, if more than one should prove to have been implicated, "for the conviction of any one of the assassins." In the proclamation setting forth this reward, a full pardon was promised to any accomplice who should come forward in evidence against his fellow; and to the whole was appended, wherever it appeared, the private placard of a committee of citizens, offering ten thousand francs, in addition to the amount proposed by the Prefecture. The entire reward thus stood at no less than thirty thousand francs, which will be regarded as an extraordinary sum when we consider the humble condition of the girl, and the great frequency in large cities, of such atrocities as the one described.

No one doubted now that the mystery of this murder would be immediately brought to light. But although, in one or two instances, arrests were made which promised elucidation, yet nothing was elicited which could implicate the parties suspected; and they were discharged forthwith. Strange as it may appear, the third week from the discovery of the body had passed, and passed without any light being thrown upon the subject, before even a rumor of the events which had so agitated the public mind, reached the ears of Dupin and myself. Engaged in researches which had absorbed our whole attention, it had been nearly a month since either of us had gone abroad, or received a visitor, or more than glanced at the leading political articles in one of

[handwritten margin notes: "not real world but a character's face", "Dupin hears about it", "the murder"]

the daily papers. The first intelligence of the murder was brought us by G—, in person. He called upon us early in the afternoon of the thirteenth of July, 18—, and remained with us until late in the night. He had been piqued by the failure of all his endeavors to ferret out the assassins. His reputation—so he said with a peculiarly Parisian air—was at stake. Even his honor was concerned. The eyes of the public were upon him; and there was really no sacrifice which he would not be willing to make for the development of the mystery. He concluded a somewhat droll speech with a compliment upon what he was pleased to term the tact of Dupin, and made him a direct, and certainly a liberal proposition, the precise nature of which I do not feel myself at liberty to disclose, but which has no bearing upon the proper subject of my narrative.

Krish is a dude
was is
here awesome at

The compliment my friend rebutted as best he could, but the proposition he accepted at once, although its advantages were altogether provisional. This point being settled, the Prefect broke forth at once into explanations of his own views, interspersing them with long comments upon the evidence; of which latter we were not yet in possession. He discoursed much, and beyond doubt, learnedly; while I hazarded an occasional suggestion as the night wore drowsily away. Dupin, sitting steadily in his accustomed arm-chair, was the embodiment of respectful attention. He wore spectacles, during the whole interview; and an occasional glance beneath their green glasses, sufficed to convince me that he slept not the less soundly, because silently, throughout the seven or eight leaden-footed hours which immediately preceded the departure of the Prefect.

In the morning, I procured, at the
Prefecture, a full report of all the
evidence elicited, and, at the various
newspaper offices, a copy of every paper
in which, from first to last, had been
published any decisive information in
regard to this sad affair. Freed from all
that was positively disproved, this mass
of information stood thus:

Marie Rogêt left the residence of her
mother, in the Rue Pavée vée St. Andrée,
about nine o'clock in the morning of
Sunday, June the twenty-second, 18—.
In going out, she gave notice to a
Monsieur Jacques St. Eustache, and to
him only, of her intention to spend the
day with an aunt who resided in the Rue
des Drômes. The Rue des Drômes is a
short and narrow but populous
thoroughfare, not far from the banks of
the river, and at a distance of some two

miles, in the most direct course possible, from the pension of Madame Rogêt. St. Eustache was the accepted suitor of Marie, and lodged, as well as took his meals, at the pension. He was to have gone for his betrothed at dusk, and to have escorted her home. In the afternoon, however, it came on to rain heavily; and, supposing that she would remain all night at her aunt's, (as she had done under similar circumstances before,) he did not think it necessary to keep his promise. As night drew on, Madame Rogêt (who was an infirm old lady, seventy years of age,) was heard to express a fear "that she should never see Marie again;" but this observation attracted little attention at the time.

On Monday, it was ascertained that the girl had not been to the Rue des Drômes; and when the day elapsed without tidings of her, a tardy search was instituted at several points in the city, and its environs. It was not, however, until the fourth day from the period of her disappearance that anything satisfactory was ascertained respecting her. On this day, (Wednesday, the twenty-fifth of June,) a Monsieur Beauvais, who, with a friend, had been making inquiries for Marie near the Barrière du Roule, on the shore of the Seine which is opposite the Rue Pavée St. Andrée, was informed that a corpse had just been towed ashore by some fishermen, who had found it floating in the river. Upon seeing the body, Beauvais, after some hesitation, identified it as that of the perfumery-girl. His friend recognized it more promptly.

The face was suffused with dark blood, some of which issued from the mouth. No foam was seen, as in the case of the merely drowned. There was no discoloration in the cellular tissue. About the throat were bruises and impressions of fingers. The arms were bent over on the chest and were rigid. The right hand was clenched; the left partially open. On the left wrist were two circular excoriations, apparently the effect of ropes, or of a rope in more than one volution. A part of the right wrist, also, was much chafed, as well as the back throughout its extent, but more especially at the shoulder-blades. In bringing the body to the shore the fishermen had attached to it a rope; but none of the excoriations had been effected by this. The flesh of the neck was much swollen. There were no cuts apparent, or bruises which appeared the effect of blows. A piece of lace was found tied so tightly around the neck as to be hidden from sight; it was completely buried in the flesh, and was fastened by a knot which lay just under the left ear. This alone would have sufficed to produce death. The medical testimony spoke confidently of the virtuous character of the deceased. She had been subjected, it said, to brutal violence. The corpse was in such condition when found, that there could have been no difficulty in its recognition by friends.

The dress was much torn and otherwise disordered. In the outer garment, a slip, about a foot wide, had been torn upward from the bottom hem to the waist, but not torn off. It was wound three times around the waist, and secured by a sort of hitch in the back. The dress immediately beneath the frock was of fine muslin; and from this a slip eighteen inches wide had been torn entirely out—torn very evenly and with great care. It was found around her neck, fitting loosely, and secured with a hard knot. Over this muslin slip and the slip of lace, the strings of a bonnet were attached; the bonnet being appended. The knot by which the strings of the bonnet were fastened, was not a lady's, but a slip or sailor's knot.

After the recognition of the corpse, it was not, as usual, taken to the Morgue, (this formality being superfluous,) but hastily interred not far from the spot at which it was brought ashore. Through the exertions of Beauvais, the matter was industriously hushed up, as far as possible; and several days had elapsed before any public emotion resulted. A weekly paper, however, at length took up the theme; the corpse was disinterred, and a re-examination instituted; but nothing was elicited beyond what has been already noted. The clothes, however, were now submitted to the mother and friends of the deceased, and fully identified as those worn by the girl upon leaving home.

Meantime, the excitement increased hourly. Several individuals were arrested and discharged. St. Eustache fell especially under suspicion; and he failed, at first, to give an intelligible account of his whereabouts during the Sunday on which Marie left home. Subsequently, however, he submitted to Monsieur G—, affidavits, accounting satisfactorily for every hour of the day in question. As time passed and no discovery ensued, a thousand contradictory rumors were circulated, and journalists busied themselves in suggestions. Among these, the one which attracted the most notice, was the idea that Marie Rogêt still lived— that the corpse found in the Seine was that of some other unfortunate. It will be proper that I submit to the reader some passages which embody the suggestion alluded to. These passages are literal translations from L'Etoile, a paper conducted, in general, with much ability.

"Mademoiselle Rogêt left her mother's house on Sunday morning, June the twenty-second, 18—, with the ostensible purpose of going to see her aunt, or some other connection, in the Rue des Drômes. From that hour, nobody is proved to have seen her. There is no trace or tidings of her at all... There has no person, whatever, come forward, so far, who saw her at all, on that day, after she left her mother's door... Now, though we have no evidence that Marie Rogêt was in the land of the living after nine o'clock on Sunday, June the twenty-second, we have proof that, up to that hour, she was alive. On Wednesday noon, at twelve, a female body was discovered afloat on the shore of the Barrière du Roule. This was, even if we presume that Marie Rogêt was thrown into the river within three hours after she left her mother's house, only three days from the time she left her home— three days to an hour. But it is folly to suppose that the murder, if murder was committed on her body, could have been consummated soon enough to have enabled her murderers to throw the body into the river before midnight. Those who are guilty of such horrid crimes, choose darkness rather than light... Thus we see that if the body found in the river was that of Marie Rogêt, it could only have been in the water two and a half days, or three at the outside. All experience has shown that drowned bodies, or bodies thrown into the water immediately after death by violence, require from six to ten days for sufficient decomposition to take place to

bring them to the top of the water. Even
where a cannon is fired over a corpse,
and it rises before at least five or six
days' immersion, it sinks again, if let
alone. Now, we ask, what was there in
this case to cause a departure from the
ordinary course of nature?... If the body
had been kept in its mangled state on
shore until Tuesday night, some trace
would be found on shore of the
murderers. It is a doubtful point, also,
whether the body would be so soon
afloat, even were it thrown in after
having been dead two days. And,
furthermore, it is exceedingly
improbable that any villains, who had
committed such a murder as is here
supposed, would have thrown the body
in without weight to sink it, when such a
precaution could have so easily been
taken."

The editor here proceeds to argue that
the body must have been in the water
"not three days merely, but, at least, five
times three days," because it was so far
decomposed that Beauvais had great
difficulty in recognizing it. This latter
point, however, was fully disproved. I
continue the translation:

"What, then, are the facts on which M.
Beauvais says that he has no doubt the
body was that of Marie Rogêt? He
ripped up the gown sleeve, and says he
found marks which satisfied him of the
identity. The public generally supposed
those marks to have consisted of some
description of scars. He rubbed the arm
and found hair upon it—something as
indefinite, we think, as can readily be
imagined—as little conclusive as finding
an arm in the sleeve. M. Beauvais did
not return that night, but sent word to
Madame Rogêt, at seven o'clock, on

Wednesday evening, that an investigation was still in progress respecting her daughter. If we allow that Madame Rogêt, from her age and grief, could not go over, (which is allowing a great deal,) there certainly must have been someone who would have thought it worthwhile to go over and attend the investigation, if they thought the body was that of Marie Nobody went over. There was nothing said or heard about the matter in the Rue Pavée St. Andrée, that reached even the occupants of the same building. M. St. Eustache, the lover and intended husband of Marie, who boarded in her mother's house, deposes that he did not hear of the discovery of the body of his intended until the next morning, when M. Beauvais came into his chamber and told him of it. For an item of news like this, it strikes us it was very coolly received."

In this way the journal endeavored to create the impression of an apathy on the part of the relatives of Marie, inconsistent with the supposition that these relatives believed the corpse to be hers. Its insinuations amount to this:— that Marie, with the connivance of her friends, had absented herself from the city for reasons involving a charge against her chastity; and that these friends, upon the discovery of a corpse in the Seine, somewhat resembling that of the girl, had availed themselves of the opportunity to impress the public with the belief of her death. But L'Etoile was again over-hasty. It was distinctly proved that no apathy, such as was imagined, existed; that the old lady was exceedingly feeble, and so agitated as to be unable to attend to any duty; that St. Eustache, so far from receiving the news coolly, was distracted with grief, and bore himself so frantically, that M.

Beauvais prevailed upon a friend and relative to take charge of him, and prevent his attending the examination at the disinterment. Moreover, although it was stated by L'Etoile, that the corpse was re-interred at the public expense—that an advantageous offer of private sepulture was absolutely declined by the family—and that no member of the family attended the ceremonial:—although, I say, all this was asserted by L'Etoile in furtherance of the impression it designed to convey—yet all this was satisfactorily disproved. In a subsequent number of the paper, an attempt was made to throw suspicion upon Beauvais himself. The editor says:

"Now, then, a change comes over the matter. We are told that, on one occasion, while a Madame B—was at Madame Rogêt's house, M. Beauvais, who was going out, told her that a gendarme was expected there, and that she, Madame B., must not say anything to the gendarme until he returned, but let the matter be for him. In the present posture of affairs, M. Beauvais appears to have the whole matter locked up in his head. A single step cannot be taken without M. Beauvais; for, go which way you will, you run against him. For some reason, he determined that nobody shall have anything to do with the proceedings but himself, and he has elbowed the male relatives out of the way, according to their representations, in a very singular manner. He seems to have been very much averse to permitting the relatives to see the body."

By the following fact, some color was given to the suspicion thus thrown upon Beauvais. A visitor at his office, a few days prior to the girl's disappearance, and during the absence of its occupant, had observed a rose in the key-hole of the door, and the name " Marie" inscribed upon a slate which hung near at hand.

The general impression, so far as we were enabled to glean it from the newspapers, seemed to be, that Marie had been the victim tim of a gang of desperadoes—that by these she had been borne across the river, maltreated and murdered. Le Commerciel, however, a print of extensive influence, was earnest in combating this popular idea. I quote a passage or two from its columns:

"We are persuaded that pursuit has hitherto been on a false scent, so far as it has been directed to the Barrière du Roule. It is impossible that a person so well known to thousands as this young woman was, should have passed three blocks without someone having seen

her; and any one who saw her would
have remembered it, for she interested
all who knew her. It was when the
streets were full of people, when she
went out. It is impossible that she could
have gone to the Barrière du Roule, or to
the Rue des Dromes, without being
recognized by a dozen persons; yet no
one has come forward who saw her
outside of her mother's door, and there
is no evidence, except the testimony
concerning her expressed intentions,
that she did go out at all. Her gown was
torn, bound round her, and tied; and by
that the body was carried as a bundle. If
the murder had been committed at the
Barrière du Roule, there would have
been no necessity for any such
arrangement. The fact that the body was
found floating near the Barrière, is no
proof as to where it was thrown into the
water. A piece of one of the unfortunate
girl's petticoats, two feet long and one

foot wide, was torn out and tied under her chin around the back of her head, probably to prevent screams. This was done by fellows who had no pocket-handkerchief."

A day or two before the Perfect called upon us, however, some important information reached the police, which seemed to overthrow, at least, the chief portion of Le Commerciel's argument. Two small boys, sons of a Madame Deluc, while roaming among the woods near the Barrière du Roule, chanced to penetrate a close thicket, within which were three or four large stones, forming a kind of seat, with a back and footstool. On the upper stone lay a white petticoat; on the second a silk scarf. A parasol, gloves, and a pocket-handkerchief were also here found. The handkerchief bore the name "Marie Rogêt." Fragments of dress were discovered on the brambles around. The earth was trampled, the bushes were broken, and there was every evidence of a struggle. Between the thicket and the river, the fences were found taken down, and the ground bore evidence of some heavy burthen having been dragged along it.

A weekly paper, Le Soleil, had the following comments upon this discovery—comments which merely echoed the sentiment of the whole Parisian press:

"The things had all evidently been there at least three or four weeks; they were all mildewed down hard with the action of the rain, and stuck together from mildew. The grass had grown around and over some of them. The silk on the parasol was strong, but the threads of it were run together within. The upper part, where it had been doubled and folded, was all mildewed and rotten, and tore on its being opened. The pieces of her frock torn out by the bushes were about three inches wide and six inches long. One part was the hem of the frock, and it had been mended; the other piece was part of the skirt, not the hem. They looked like strips torn off, and were on the thorn bush, about a foot from the ground. There can be no doubt, therefore, that the spot of this appalling outrage has been discovered."

Consequent upon this discovery, new evidence appeared. Madame Deluc testified that she keeps a roadside inn not far from the bank of the river, opposite the Barrière du Roule. The neighborhood is secluded—particularly so. It is the usual Sunday resort of blackguards from the city, who cross the river in boats. About three o'clock, in the afternoon of the Sunday in question, a young girl arrived at the inn, accompanied by a young man of dark complexion. The two remained here for some time. On their departure, they took the road to some thick woods in the vicinity. Madame Deluc's attention was called to the dress worn by the girl, on account of its resemblance to one worn by a deceased relative. A scarf was particularly noticed. Soon after the departure of the couple, a gang of miscreants made their appearance, behaved boisterously, ate and drank without making payment, followed in the route of the young man and girl, returned to the inn about dusk, and re-crossed the river as if in great haste.

It was soon after dark, upon this same evening, that Madame Deluc, as well as her eldest son, heard the screams of a female in the vicinity of the inn. The screams were violent but brief. Madame

D. recognized not only the scarf which was found in the thicket, but the dress which was discovered upon the corpse. An omnibus-driver, Valence, now also testified that he saw Marie Rogêt cross a ferry on the Seine, on the Sunday in question, in company with a young man of dark complexion. He, Valence, knew Marie, and could not be mistaken in her identity. The articles found in the thicket were fully identified by the relatives of Marie.

The items of evidence and information thus collected by myself, from the newspapers, at the suggestion of Dupin, embraced only one more point—but this was a point of seemingly vast consequence. It appears that, immediately after the discovery of the clothes as above described, the lifeless, or nearly lifeless body of St. Eustache, Marie's betrothed, was found in the vicinity of what all now supposed the scene of the outrage. A phial labeled "laudanum," and emptied, was found near him. His breath gave evidence of the poison. He died without speaking. Upon his person was found a letter, briefly stating his love for Marie, with his design of self-destruction.

"I need scarcely tell you," said Dupin, as he finished the perusal of my notes, "that this is a far more intricate case than that of the Rue Morgue; from which it differs in one important respect. This is an ordinary, although an atrocious instance of crime. There is nothing peculiarly outré about it. You will observe that, for this reason, the mystery has been considered easy, when, for this reason, it should have been considered difficult, of solution. Thus, at first, it was thought unnecessary to offer a reward. The myrmidons of G—were able at once to comprehend how and why such an atrocity might have been committed. They could picture to their imaginations a mode—many modes—and a motive—many motives; and because it was not impossible that either of these numerous modes and motives could have been the actual one, they have taken it for granted that one of them must. But the ease with which these variable fancies were entertained, and the very plausibility which each assumed, should have been understood as indicative rather of the difficulties than of the facilities which must attend elucidation. I have before observed that it is by prominences above the plane of the ordinary nary, that reason feels her way, if at all, in her search for the true, and that the proper question in cases such as this, is not so much 'what has occurred?' as 'what has occurred that has never occurred before?' In the investigations at the house of Madame L'Espanaye, the agents of G—were discouraged and confounded by that very unusualness which, to a properly regulated intellect, would have afforded the surest omen of success; while this same intellect might have been plunged in despair at the ordinary character of all that met the eye in the case of the perfumery-girl, and yet told of nothing but easy triumph to the functionaries of the Prefecture.

"In the case of Madame L'Espanaye and her daughter, there was, even at the beginning of our investigation, no doubt that murder had been committed. The idea of suicide was excluded at once. Here, too, we are freed, at the commencement, from all supposition of self-murder. The body found at the Barrière du Roule, was found under such circumstances as to leave us no room for embarrassment upon this important point. But it has been suggested that the corpse discovered, is not that of the Marie Rogêt for the conviction of whose assassin, or assassins, the reward is offered, and respecting whom, solely, our agreement has been arranged with the Prefect. We both know this gentleman well. It will not do to trust him too far. If, dating our inquiries from the body found, and thence tracing a murderer, we yet discover this body to be that of some other individual than Marie; or, if starting from the living Marie, we find her, yet find her unassassinated—in either case we lose our labor; since it is Monsieur G—with whom we have to deal. For our own purpose, therefore, if not for the purpose of justice, it is indispensable that our first step should be the determination of the identity of

the corpse with the Marie Rogêt who is
missing.

"With the public the arguments of
L'Etoile have had weight; and that the
journal itself is convinced of their
importance would appear from the
manner in which it commences one of
its essays upon the subject—'Several of
the morning papers of the day,' it says,
'speak of the conclusive article in
Monday's Etoile.' To me, this article
appears conclusive of little beyond the
zeal of its inditer. We should bear in
mind that, in general, it is the object of
our newspapers rather to create a
sensation—to make a point—than to
further the cause of truth. The latter end
is only pursued when it seems
coïncident with the former. The print
which merely falls in with ordinary
opinion (however well founded this
opinion may be) earns for itself no credit

with the mob. The mass of the people regard as profound only him who suggests pungent contradictions of the general idea. In ratiocination, not less than in literature, it is the epigram which is the most immediately and the most universally appreciated. In both, it is of the lowest order of merit.

"What I mean to say is, that it is the mingled epigram and melodrame of the idea, that Marie Rogêt still lives, rather than any true plausibility in this idea, which have suggested it to L'Etoile, and secured it a favorable reception with the public. Let us examine the heads of this journal's argument; endeavoring to avoid the incoherence with which it is originally set forth.

"The first aim of the writer is to show, from the brevity of the interval between Marie's disappearance and the finding of the floating corpse, that this corpse cannot be that of Marie. The reduction of this interval to its smallest possible dimension, becomes thus, at once, an object with the reasoner. In the rash pursuit of this object, he rushes into mere assumption at the outset. 'It is folly to suppose,' he says, 'that the murder, if murder was committed on her body, could have been consummated soon enough to have enabled her murderers to throw the body into the river before midnight.' We demand at once, and very naturally, why? Why is it folly to suppose that the murder was committed within five minutes after the girl's quitting her mother's house? Why is it folly to suppose that the murder was committed at any given period of the day? There have been assassinations at all hours. But, had the murder taken place at any moment between nine o'clock in the morning of Sunday, and a quarter before midnight, there would still have been time enough 'to throw the body into the river before midnight.' This assumption, then, amounts precisely to this—that the murder was not committed on Sunday at all—and, if we allow L'Etoile to assume this, we may permit it any liberties whatever. The paragraph beginning 'It is folly to suppose that the murder, etc.,' however it appears as printed in L'Etoile, may be imagined to have existed actually thus in the brain of its inditer—'It is folly to suppose that the murder, if murder was committed on the body, could have been committed soon enough to have enabled her murderers to throw the body into the river before midnight; it is folly, we say, to suppose all this, and to suppose at the same time, (as we are resolved to suppose,) that the body was not thrown in until after midnight'—a sentence sufficiently inconsequential in itself, but not so utterly preposterous as the one printed.

"Were it my purpose," continued Dupin, "merely to make out a case against this passage of L'Etoile's argument, I might safely leave it where it is. It is not, however, with L'Etoile that we have to do, but with the truth. The sentence in question has but one meaning, as it stands; and this meaning I have fairly stated: but it is material that we go behind the mere words, for an idea which these words have obviously intended, and failed to convey. It was the design of the journalist to say that, at whatever period of the day or night of Sunday this murder was committed, it was improbable that the assassins would have ventured to bear the corpse to the river before midnight. And herein lies, really, the assumption of which I complain. It is assumed that the murder

was committed at such a position, and
under such circumstances, that the
bearing it to the river became necessary.
Now, the assassination might have taken
place upon the river's brink, or on the
river itself; and, thus, the throwing the
corpse in the water might have been
resorted to, at any period of the day or
night, as the most obvious and most
immediate mode of disposal. You will
understand that I suggest nothing here
as probable, or as coincident with my
own opinion. My design, so far, has no
reference to the facts of the case. I wish
merely to caution you against the whole
tone of L'Etoile's suggestion, by calling
your attention to its ex parte character at
the outset.

"Having prescribed thus a limit to suit
its own preconceived notions; having
assumed that, if this were the body of
Marie, it could have been in the water

but a very brief time; the journal goes on to say:

'All experience has shown that drowned bodies, or bodies thrown into the water immediately after death by violence, require from six to ten days for sufficient decomposition to take place to bring them to the top of the water. Even when a cannon is fired over a corpse, and it rises before at least five or six days' immersion, it sinks again if let alone.'

"These assertions have been tacitly received by every paper in Paris, with the exception of Le Moniteur. This latter print endeavors to combat that portion of the paragraph which has reference to 'drowned bodies' only, by citing some five or six instances in which the bodies of individuals known to be drowned were found floating after the lapse of less time than is insisted upon by L'Etoile. But there is something excessively unphilosophical in the attempt on the part of Le Moniteur, to rebut the general assertion of L'Etoile, by a citation of particular instances militating against that assertion. Had it been possible to adduce fifty instead of five examples of bodies found floating at the end of two or three days, these fifty examples could still have been properly regarded only as exceptions to L'Etoile's rule, until such time as the rule itself should be confuted. Admitting the rule, (and this Le Moniteur does not deny, insisting merely upon its exceptions,) the argument of L'Etoile is suffered to remain in full force; for this argument does not pretend to involve more than a question of the probability of the body having risen to the surface in less than three days; and this probability will be in favor of L'Etoile's position until the instances so childishly adduced shall be sufficient in number to establish an antagonistical rule.

"You will see at once that all argument upon this head should be urged, if at all, against the rule itself; and for this end we must examine the rationale of the rule. Now the human body, in general, is neither much lighter nor much heavier than the water of the Seine; that is to say, the specific gravity of the human body, in its natural condition, is about equal to the bulk of fresh water which it displaces. The bodies of fat and fleshy persons, with small bones, and of women generally are lighter than those of the lean and large-boned, and of men; and the specific gravity of the water of a river is somewhat influenced by the presence of the tide from sea. But, leaving this tide out of question, it may be said that very few human bodies will sink at all, even in fresh water, of their own accord . Almost any one, falling into a river, will be enabled to float, if he suffer the specific gravity of the water fairly to be adduced in comparison with his own—that is to say, if he suffer his whole person to be immersed, with as little exception as possible. The proper position for one who cannot swim, is the upright position of the walker on land, with the head thrown fully back, and immersed; the mouth and nostrils alone remaining above the surface. Thus circumstanced, we shall find that we float without difficulty and without exertion. It is evident, however, that the gravities of the body, and of the bulk of water displaced, are very nicely balanced, and that a trifle will cause either to preponderate. An arm, for instance, uplifted from the water, and thus deprived of its support, is an additional weight sufficient to immerse the whole head, while the accidental aid of the smallest piece of timber will enable us to elevate the head so as to look about. Now, in the struggles of one unused to swimming, the arms are invariably thrown upwards, while an attempt is made to keep the head in its usual perpendicular position. The result is the immersion of the mouth and nostrils, and the inception, during efforts to breathe while beneath the surface, of water into the lungs. Much is also received into the stomach, and the whole body becomes heavier by the difference between the weight of the air originally distending these cavities, and that of the fluid which now fills them. This difference is sufficient to cause the body to sink, as a general rule; but is insufficient in the cases of individuals with small bones and an abnormal quantity of flaccid or fatty matter. Such individuals float even after drowning.

"The corpse, being supposed at the bottom of the river, will there remain until, by some means, its specific gravity again becomes less than that of the bulk of water which it displaces. This effect is brought about by decomposition, or otherwise. The result of decomposition is the generation of gas, distending the cellular tissues and all the cavities, and giving the puffed appearance which is to horrible. When this distension has so far progressed that the bulk of the corpse is materially increased without a corresponding increase of mass or weight, its specific gravity becomes less than that of the water displaced, and it forthwith makes its appearance at the surface. But decomposition is modified by innumerable circumstances—is hastened or retarded by innumerable agencies; for example, by the heat or cold of the season, by the mineral impregnation or purity of the water, by its depth or shallowness, by its currency or stagnation, by the temperament of the body, by its infection or freedom from disease before death. Thus it is evident that we can assign no period, with any thing like accuracy, at which the corpse shall rise through decomposition. Under certain conditions this result would be brought about within an hour; under others, it might not take place at all. There are chemical infusions by which the animal frame can be preserved forever from corruption; the Bi-chloride of Mercury is one. But, apart from decomposition, there may be, and very usually is, a generation of gas within the stomach, from the acetous fermentation of vegetable matter (or within other cavities from other causes) sufficient to induce a distension which will bring the body to the surface. The effect produced by the firing of a cannon is that of simple vibration. This may either loosen the corpse from the soft mud or ooze in which it is imbedded, thus permitting it to rise when other agencies have already prepared it for so doing; or it may overcome the tenacity of some putrescent portions of the cellular tissue; allowing the cavities to distend under the influence of the gas.

"Having thus before us the whole philosophy of this subject, we can easily test by it the assertions of L'Etoile. 'All experience shows,' says this paper, 'that drowned bodies, or bodies thrown into the water immediately after death by violence, require from six to ten days for sufficient decomposition to take place to bring them to the top of the water. Even when a cannon is fired over a corpse, and it rises before at least five or six days' immersion, it sinks again if let alone.'

"The whole of this paragraph must now appear a tissue of inconsequence and incoherence. All experience does not show that 'drowned bodies' require from six to ten days for sufficient decomposition to take place to bring them to the surface. Both science and experience show that the period of their rising is, and necessarily must be, indeterminate. If, moreover, a body has risen to the surface through firing of cannon, it will not 'sink again if let alone,' until decomposition has so far progressed as to permit the escape of the generated gas. But I wish to call your attention to the distinction which is made between 'drowned bodies,' and 'bodies thrown into the water immediately after death by violence.'

Although the writer admits the distinction, he yet includes them all in the same category. I have shown how it is that the body of a drowning man becomes specifically heavier than its bulk of water, and that he would not sink at all, except for the struggles by which he elevates his arms above the surface, and his gasps for breath while beneath the surface— gasps which supply by water the place of the original air in the lungs. But these struggles and these gasps would not occur in the body 'thrown into the water immediately after death by violence. ' Thus, in the latter instance, the body, as a general rule, would not sink at all—a fact of which L'Etoile is evidently ignorant. When decompsition had proceeded to a very great extent— when the flesh had in a great measure left the bones—then, indeed, but not till then, should we lose sight of the corpse.

"And now what are we to make of the argument, that the body found could not be that of Marie Rogêt, because, three days only having elapsed, this body was found floating? If drowned, being a woman, she might never have sunk; or having sunk, might have re-appeared in twenty-four hours, or less. But no one supposes her to have been drowned; and, dying before being thrown into the river, she might have been found floating at any period afterwards whatever.

" 'But,' says L'Etoile, 'if the body had been kept in its mangled state on shore until Tuesday night, some trace would be found on shore of the murderers.' Here it is at first difficult to perceive the intention of the reasoner. He means to anticipate what he imagines would be an objection to his theory—viz: that the body was kept on shore two days, suffering rapid decomposition— more rapid than if immersed in water. He supposes that, had this been the case, it might have appeared at the surface on the Wednesday, and thinks that only under such circumstances it could so have appeared. He is accordingly in haste to show that it was not kept on shore; for, if so, 'some trace would be found on shore of the murderers.' I presume you smile at the sequitur. You cannot be made to see how the mere duration of the corpse on the shore could operate to multiply traces of the assassins. Nor can I.

"'And furthermore it is exceedingly improbable,' continues our journal, 'that any villains who had committed such a murder as is here supposed, would have thrown the body in without weight to sink it, when such a precaution could have so easily been taken.' Observe, here, the laughable confusion of thought! No one—not even L'Etoile—disputes the murder committed on the body found. The marks of violence are too obvious. It is our reasoner's object merely to show that this body is not Marie's. He wishes to prove that Marie is not assassinated—not that the corpse was not. Yet his observation proves only the latter point. Here is a corpse without weight attached. Murderers, casting it in, would not have failed to attach a weight. Therefore it was not thrown in by murderers. This is all which is proved, if anything is. The question of identity is not even approached, and L'Etoile has been at great pains merely to gainsay now what it has admitted only a moment before. 'We are perfectly convinced, ' it says, 'that the body found was that of a murdered female. '

"Nor is this the sole instance, even in this division of his subject, where our reasoner unwittingly reasons against himself. His evident object, I have already said, is to reduce, as much as possible, the interval between Marie's disappearance and the finding of the corpse. Yet we find him urging the point that no person saw the girl from the moment of her leaving her mother's house. 'We have no evidence,' he says, 'that Marie Rogêt was in the land of the living after nine o'clock on Sunday, June the twenty-second.' As his argument is obviously an ex parte one, he should, at least, have left this matter out of sight; for had any one been known to see Marie, say on Monday, or on Tuesday, the interval in question would have been much reduced, and, by his own ratiocination, the probability much diminished of the corpse being that of the grisette. It is, nevertheless, amusing to observe that L'Etoile insists upon its point in the full belief of its furthering its general argument.

"Reperuse now that portion of this argument which has reference to the identification of the corpse by Beauvais. In regard to the hair upon the arm, L'Etoile has been obviously disingenuous. M. Beauvais, not being an idiot, could never have urged, in identification of the corpse, simply hair upon its arm. No arm is without hair. The generality of the expression of L'Etoile is a mere perversion of the witness' phraseology. He must have spoken of some peculiarity in this hair. It must have been a peculiarity of color, of quantity, of length, or of situation.

"'Her foot,' says the journal, 'was small—so are thousands of feet. Her garter is no proof whatever—nor is her shoe—for shoes and garters are sold in packages. The same may be said of the flowers in her hat. One thing upon which M. Beauvais strongly insists is, that the clasp on the garter found, had been set back to take it in. This amounts to nothing; for most women find it proper to take a pair of garters home and fit them to the size of the limbs they are to encircle, rather than to try them in the store where they purchase.' Here it is difficult to suppose the reasoner in earnest. Had M. Beauvais, in his search for the body of Marie, discovered a corpse corresponding in general size and appearance to the missing girl, he would have been warranted (without reference to the question of habiliment at all) in forming an opinion that his search had been successful. If, in addition to the point of general size and contour, he had found upon the arm a peculiar hairy appearance which he had observed upon the living Marie, his opinion might have been justly strengthened; and the increase of positiveness might well have been in the ratio of the peculiarity, or unusualness, of the hairy mark. If, the feet of Marie being small, those of the corpse were also small, the increase of probability that the body was that of Marie would not be an increase in a ratio merely arithmetical, but in one highly geometrical, or accumulative. Add to all this shoes such as she had been known to wear upon the day of her disappearance, and, although these shoes may be 'sold in packages,' you so far augment the probability as to verge upon the certain. What, of itself, would be no evidence of identity, becomes through its corroborative position, proof most sure. Give us, then, flowers in the hat corresponding to those worn by the missing girl, and we seek for nothing farther. If only one flower, we seek for nothing farther—what then if two or three, or more? Each successive one is multiple evidence—proof not added to proof, but multiplied by hundreds or thousands. Let us now discover, upon the deceased, garters such as the living used, and it is almost folly to proceed. But these garters are found to be tightened, by the setting back of a clasp, in just such a manner as her own had been tightened by Marie, shortly previous to her leaving home. It is now madness or hypocrisy to doubt. What L'Etoile says in respect to this abbreviation of the garter's being an usual occurrence, shows nothing beyond its own pertinacity in error. The elastic nature of the clasp-garter is self-demonstration of the unusualness of the abbreviation. What is made to adjust itself, must of necessity require foreign adjustment but rarely. It must have been by an accident, in its strictest sense, that these garters of Marie needed the tightening described. They alone would have amply established her identity. But it is not that the corpse was found to have the garters of the missing girl, or found to have her shoes, or her bonnet, or the flowers of her bonnet, or her feet, or a peculiar mark upon the arm, or her general size and appearance— it is that the corpse had each, and all collectively. Could it be proved that the editor of L'Etoile really entertained a doubt, under the circumstances, there would be no need, in his case, of a commission de lunatico inquirendo. He has thought it sagacious to echo the small talk of the lawyers, who, for the most part, content themselves with echoing the rectangular precepts of the courts. I would here observe that very much of what is rejected as evidence by a court, is the best of evidence to the intellect. For the court, guiding itself by the general principles of evidence— the recognized and booked principles—is averse from swerving at particular instances. And this steadfast adherence to principle, with rigorous disregard of the conflicting exception, is a sure mode of attaining the maximum of attainable truth, in any long sequence of time. The practice, in mass, is therefore philosophical ical; but it is not the less certain that it engenders vast individual error.

"In respect to the insinuations leveled at Beauvais, you will be willing to dismiss them in a breath. You have already fathomed the true character of this good gentleman. He is a busy-body, with much of romance and little of wit. Any one so constituted will readily so conduct himself, upon occasion of real excitement, as to render himself liable to suspicion on the part of the over-acute, or the ill-disposed. M. Beauvais (as it appears from your notes) had some personal interviews with the editor of L'Etoile, and offended him by venturing an opinion that the corpse, notwithstanding the theory of the editor, was, in sober fact, that of Marie. 'He persists,' says the paper, 'in asserting the corpse to be that of Marie, but cannot give a circumstance, in addition to those which we have commented upon, to make others believe.' Now, without re-adverting to the fact that stronger evidence 'to make others believe,' could never have been adduced, it may be remarked that a man may very well be understood to believe, in a case of this kind, without the ability to advance a single reason for the belief of a second party. Nothing is more vague than impressions of individual identity. Each man recognizes his neighbor, yet there are few instances in which any one is prepared to give a reason for his recognition. The editor of L'Etoile had no right to be offended at M. Beauvais' unreasoning belief.

"The suspicious circumstances which invest him, will be found to tally much better with my hypothesis of romantic busy-bodyism, then with the reasoner's suggestion of guilt. Once adopting the more charitable interpretation, we shall find no difficulty in comprehending the rose in the key-hole; the 'Marie' upon the slate; the 'elbowing the male relatives out of the way;' the 'aversion to permitting them to see the body;' the caution given to Madame B—, that she must hold no conversation with the gendarme until his return (Beauvais'); and, lastly, his apparent determination 'that nobody should have anything to do with the proceedings except himself.' It seems to me unquestionable that

Beauvais was a suitor of Marie's; that she coquetted with him; and that he was ambitious of being thought to enjoy her fullest intimacy and confidence. I shall say nothing more upon this point; and, as the evidence fully rebuts the assertion of L'Etoile, touching the matter of apathy on the part of the mother and other relatives—an apathy inconsistent with the supposition of their believing the corpse to be that of the perfumery-girl—we shall now proceed as if the question of identity were settled to our perfect satisfaction."

"And what," I here demanded, "do you think of the opinions of Le Commerciel?"

"That, in spirit, they are far more worthy of attention than any which have been promulgated upon the subject. The deductions from the premises are philosophical and acute; but the premises, in two instances, at least, are founded in imperfect observation. Le Commerciel wishes to intimate that Marie was seized by some gang of low ruffians not far from her mother's door. 'It is impossible,' it urges, 'that a person so well known to thousands as this young woman was, should have passed three blocks without some one having seen her.' This is the idea of a man long resident in Paris—a public man—and one whose walks to and fro in the city, have been mostly limited to the vicinity of the public offices. He is aware that he seldom passes so far as a dozen blocks from his own bureau, without being recognized and accosted. And, knowing the extent of his personal acquaintance with others, and of others with him, he compares his notoriety with that of the perfumery-girl, finds no great difference between them, and reaches at once the conclusion that she, in her walks, would be equally liable to recognition with himself in his. This could only be the case were her walks of the same unvarying, methodical character, and within the same species of limited region as are his own. He passes to and fro, at regular intervals, within a confined periphery, abounding in individuals who are led to observation of his person through interest in the kindred nature of his occupation with their own. But the walks of Marie may, in general, be supposed discursive. In this particular instance, it will be understood as most probable, that she proceeded upon a route of more than average diversity from her accustomed ones. The parallel which we imagine to have existed in the mind of Le Commercial would only be sustained in the event of the two individuals' traversing the whole city. In this case, granting the personal acquaintances to be equal, the chances would be also equal that an equal number of personal encounters would be made. For my own part, I should hold it not only as possible, but as very far more than probable, that Marie might have proceeded, at any given period, by any one of the many routes between her own residence and that of her aunt, without meeting a single individual whom she knew, or by whom she was known. In viewing this question in its full and proper light, we must hold steadily in mind the great disproportion between the personal acquaintances of even the most noted individual in Paris, and the entire population of Paris itself.

"But whatever force there may still appear to be in the suggestion of Le Commerciel, will be much diminished when we take into consideration the hour at which the girl went abroad. 'It

was when the streets were full of people,'
says Le Commerciel, 'that she went out.'
But not so. It was at nine o'clock in the
morning. Now at nine o'clock of every
morning in the week, with the exception
of Sunday, the streets of the city are, it is
true, thronged with people. At nine on
Sunday, the populace are chiefly within
doors preparing for church. No
observing person can have failed to
notice the peculiarly deserted air of the
town, from about eight until ten on the
morning of every Sabbath. Between ten
and eleven the streets are thronged, but
not at so early a period as that
designated.

"There is another point at which there
seems a deficiency of observation on the
part of Le Commerciel. 'A piece,' it says,
'of one of the unfortunate girl's
petticoats, two feet long, and one foot
wide, was torn out and tied under her

chin, and around the back of her head, probably to prevent screams. This was done by fellows who had no pocket-handkerchiefs.' Whether this idea is, or is not well founded, we will endeavor to see hereafter; but by 'fellows who have no pocket-handkerchiefs,' the editor intends the lowest class of ruffians. These, however, are the very description of people who will always be found to have handkerchiefs even when destitute of shirts. You must have had occasion to observe how absolutely indispensable, of late years, to the thorough blackguard, has become the pocket-handkerchief."

"And what are we to think," I asked, "of the article in Le Soleil?"

"That it is a vast pity its inditer was not born a parrot—in which case he would have been the most illustrious parrot of his race. He has merely repeated the individual items of the already published opinion; collecting them, with a laudable industry, from this paper and from that. 'The things had all evidently been there,' he says, 'at least, three or four weeks, and there can be no doubt that the spot of this appalling outrage has been discovered. ' The facts here re-stated by Le Soleil, are very far indeed from removing my own doubts upon this subject, and we will examine them more particularly hereafter in connexion with another division of the theme.

"At present we must occupy ourselves with other investigations. You cannot fail to have remarked the extreme laxity of the examination of the corpse. To be sure, the question of identity was readily determined, or should have been; but there were other points to be ascertained. Had the body been in any respect despoiled? Had the deceased any articles of jewelry about her person upon leaving home? if so, had she any when found? These are important questions utterly untouched by the evidence; and there are others of equal moment, which have met with no attention. We must endeavor to satisfy ourselves by personal inquiry. The case of St. Eustache must be re-examined. I have no suspicion of this person; but let us proceed methodically. We will ascertain beyond a doubt the validity of the affidavits in regard to his whereabouts on the Sunday. Affidavits of this character are readily made matter of mystification. Should there be nothing wrong here, however, we will dismiss St. Eustache from our investigations. His suicide, however corroborative of suspicion, were there found to be deceit in the affidavits, is, without such deceit, in no respect an unaccountable circumstance, or one which need cause us to deflect from the line of ordinary analysis.

"In that which I now propose, we will discard the interior points of this tragedy, and concentrate our attention upon its outskirts. Not the least usual error, in investigations such as this, is the limiting of inquiry to the immediate, with total disregard of the collateral or circumstantial events. It is the mal-practice of the courts to confine evidence and discussion to the bounds of apparent relevancy. Yet experience has shown, and a true philosophy will always show, that a vast, perhaps the larger portion of truth, arises from the seemingly irrelevant. It is through the spirit of this principle, if not precisely through its letter, that modern science has resolved to calculate upon the unforeseen. But perhaps you do not comprehend me. The history of human

knowledge has so uninterruptedly
shown that to collateral, or incidental, or
accidental events we are indebted for the
most numerous and most valuable
discoveries, that it has at length become
necessary, in any prospective view of
improvement, to make not only large,
but the largest allowances for inventions
that shall arise by chance, and quite out
of the range of ordinary expectation. It is
no longer philosophical to base, upon
what has been, a vision of what is to be.
Accident is admitted as a portion of the
substructure. We make chance a matter
of absolute calculation. We subject the
unlooked for and unimagined, to the
mathematical formulae of the schools.

"I repeat that it is no more than fact,
that the larger portion of all truth has
sprung from the collateral; and it is but
in accordance with the spirit of the
principle involved in this fact, that I

would divert inquiry, in the present case, from the trodden and hitherto unfruitful ground of the event itself, to the cotemporary circumstances which surround it. While you ascertain the validity of the affidavits, I will examine the newspapers more generally than you have as yet done. So far, we have only reconnoitered the field of investigation; but it will be strange indeed if a comprehensive survey, such as I propose, of the public prints, will not afford us some minute points which shall establish a direction for inquiry."

In pursuance of Dupin's suggestion, I made scrupulous examination of the affair of the affidavits. The result was a firm conviction of their validity, and of the consequent innocence of St. Eustache. In the mean time my friend occupied himself, with what seemed to me a minuteness altogether objectless, in a scrutiny of the various newspaper files. At the end of a week he placed before me the following extracts:

"About three years and a half ago, a disturbance very similar to the present, was caused by the disappearance of this same Marie Rogêt, from the parfumerie of Monsieur Le Blane, in the Palais Royal. At the end of a week, however, she re-appeared at her customary comptoir, as well as ever, with the exception of a slight paleness not altogether usual. It was given out by Monsieur Le Blane and her mother, that she had merely been on a visit to some friend in the country; and the affair was speedily hushed up. We presume that the present absence is a freak of the same nature, and that, at the expiration of a week, or perhaps of a month, we shall have her among us again."

—Evening Paper—Monday, June 23. "An evening journal of yesterday, refers to a former mysterious disappearance of Mademoiselle Rogêt. It is well known that, during the week of her absence from Le Blane's parfumerie, she was in the company of a young naval officer, much noted for his debaucheries. A quarrel, it is supposed, providentially led to her return home. We have the name of the Lothario in question, who is, at present, stationed in Paris, but, for obvious reasons, forbear to make it public."

—Le Mercurie—Tuesday Morning, June 24. "An outrage of the most atrocious character was perpetrated near this city the day before yesterday. A gentleman, with his wife and daughter, engaged, about dusk, the services of six young men, who were idly rowing a boat to and fro near the banks of the Seine, to

convey him across the river. Upon
reaching the opposite shore, the three
passengers stepped out, and had
proceeded so far as to be beyond the
view of the boat, when the daughter
discovered that she had left in it her
parasol. She returned for it, was seized
by the gang, carried out into the stream,
gagged, brutally treated, and finally
taken to the shore at a point not far from
that at which she had originally entered
the boat with her parents. The villains
have escaped for the time, but the police
are upon their trail, and some of them
will soon be taken."

—Morning Paper—June 25. "We have
received one or two communications,
the object of which is to fasten the crime
of the late atrocity upon Mennais; but as
this gentleman has been fully
exonerated by a legal inquiry, and as the
arguments of our several

correspondents appear to be more zealous than profound, we do not think it advisable to make them public."

—Morning Paper—June 28. "We have received several forcibly written communications, apparently from various sources, and which go far to render it a matter of certainty that the unfortunate Marie Rogêt has become a victim of one of the numerous bands of blackguards which infest the vicinity of the city upon Sunday. Our own opinion is decidedly in favor of this supposition. We shall endeavor to make room for some of these arguments hereafter."

—Evening Paper—Tuesday, June 31. "On Monday, one of the bargemen connected with the revenue service, saw an empty boat floating down the Seine. Sails were lying in the bottom of the boat. The bargeman towed it under the barge office. The next morning it was taken from thence, without the knowledge of any of the officers. The rudder is now at the barge office."

—Le Diligence—Thursday, June 26. Upon reading these various extracts, they not only seemed to me irrelevant, but I could perceive no mode in which any one of them could be brought to bear upon the matter in hand. I waited for some explanation from Dupin.

"It is not my present design," he said, "to dwell upon the first and second of these extracts. I have copied them chiefly to show you the extreme remissness of the police, who, as far as I can understand from the Prefect, have not troubled themselves, in any respect, with an examination of the naval officer alluded to. Yet it is mere folly to say that between the first and second disappearance of Marie, there is no supposable connection. Let us admit the first elopement to have resulted in a quarrel between the lovers, and the return home of the betrayed. We are now prepared to view a second elopement (if we know that an elopement has again taken place) as indicating a renewal of the betrayer's advances, rather than as the result of new proposals by a second individual— we are prepared to regard it as a 'making up' of the old amour, rather than as the commencement of a new one. The chances are ten to one, that he who had once eloped with Marie, would again propose an elopement, rather than that she to whom proposals of elopement had been made by one individual, should have them made to her by another. And here let me call your attention to the fact, that the time elapsing between the first ascertained, and the second supposed elopement, is a few months more than the general period of the cruises of our men-of-war. Had the lover been interrupted in his first villany by the necessity of departure to sea, and had he seized the first moment of his return to renew the base designs not yet altogether accomplished— or not yet altogether accomplished by him? Of all these things we know nothing.

"You will say, however, that, in the second instance, there was no elopement as imagined. Certainly not— but are we prepared to say that there was not the frustrated design? Beyond St. Eustache; and perhaps Beauvais, we find no recognized, no open, no honorable suitors of Marie. Of none other is there any thing said. Who, then, is the secret lover, of whom the relatives (at least most of them) know nothing, but whom Marie meets upon the morning of Sunday, and who is so deeply in her confidence, that she hesitates not to remain with him until the shades of the evening descend, amid the solitary groves of the Barrière du Roule? Who is that secret lover, I ask, of whom, at least, most of the relatives know nothing? And what means the singular prophecy of Madame Rogêt on the morning of Marie's departure?— 'I fear that I shall never see Marie again.'

"But if we cannot imagine Madame Rogêt privy to the design of elopement, may we not at least suppose this design entertained by the girl? Upon quitting home, she gave it to be understood that she was about to visit her aunt in the Rue des Drômes, and St. Eustache was requested to call for her at dark. Now, at first glance, this fact strongly militates against my suggestion;—but let us reflect. That she did meet some companion, and proceed with him across the river, reaching the Barrière du Roule at so late an hour as three o'clock in the afternoon, is known. But in consenting so to accompany this individual, (for whatever purpose— to her mother known or unknown,) she must have thought of her expressed intention when leaving home, and of the surprise and suspicion aroused in the bosom of her affianced suitor, St. Eustache, when, calling for her, at the hour appointed, in the Rue des Drômes, he should find that she had not been there, and when, moreover, upon returning to the pension with this alarming intelligence, he should become aware of her continued absence from home. She must have thought of these things, I say. She must have foreseen the chagrin of St. Eustache, the suspicion of all. She could not have thought of returning to brave this suspicion; but the suspicion becomes a point of trivial importance to her, if we suppose her not intending to return.

"We may imagine her thinking thus—'I am to meet a certain person for the purpose of elopement, or for certain other purposes known only to myself. It is necessary that there be no chance of interruption—there must be sufficient time given us to elude pursuit— I will give it to be understood that I shall visit and spend the day with my aunt at the Rue des Drômes—I well tell St. Eustache not to call for me until dark—in this way, my absence from home for the longest possible period, without causing suspicion or anxiety, will be accounted for, and I shall gain more time than in any other manner. If I bid St. Eustache call for me at dark, he will be sure not to call before; but, if I wholly neglect to bid him call, my time for escape will be diminished, since it will be expected that I return the earlier, and my absence will the sooner excite anxiety. Now, if it were my design to return at all—if I had in contemplation merely a stroll with the individual in question—it would not be my policy to bid St. Eustache call; for, calling, he will be sure to ascertain that I have played him false—a fact of which I might keep him for ever in ignorance, by leaving home without notifying him of my intention, by returning before dark, and by then stating that I had been to visit my aunt in the Rue des Drômes. But, as it is my design never to return— or not for some weeks—or not until certain concealments are effected—the gaining of time is the only point about which I need give myself any concern.'

"You have observed, in your notes, that the most general opinion in relation to this sad affair is, and was from the first, that the girl had been the victim of a gang of blackguards. Now, the popular opinion, under certain conditions, is not to be disregarded. When arising of itself—when manifesting itself in a strictly spontaneous manner—we should look upon it as analogous with that intuition which is the idiosyncrasy of the individual man of genius. In ninety-nine cases from the hundred I would abide by its decision. But it is important that we find no palpable traces of suggestion. The opinion must be rigorously the public's own; and the distinction is often exceedingly difficult to perceive and to maintain. In the present instance, it appears to me that this 'public opinion,' in respect to a gang, has been superinduced by the collateral event which is detailed in the third of my extracts. All Paris is excited by the discovered corpse of Marie, a girl young, beautiful and notorious. This corpse is found, bearing marks of violence, and floating in the river. But it is now made known that, at the very period, or about the very period, in which it is supposed that the girl was assassinated, an outrage similar in nature to that endured by the deceased, although less in extent, was perpetrated, by a gang of young ruffians, upon the person of a second young female. Is it wonderful that the one known atrocity should influence the popular judgment in regard to the other unknown? This judgment awaited direction, and the known outrage seemed so opportunely to afford it! Marie, too, was found in the river; and upon this very river was this known outrage committed. The connexion of the two events had about it so much of the palpable, that the true wonder would have been a failure of the populace to appreciate and to seize it.

But, in fact, the one atrocity, known to be so committed, is, if any thing, evidence that the other, committed at a time nearly coincident, was not so committed. It would have been a miracle indeed, if, while a gang of ruffians were perpetrating, at a given locality, a most unheard-of wrong, there should have been another similar gang, in a similar locality, in the same city, under the same circumstances, with the same means and appliances, engaged in a wrong of precisely the same aspect, at precisely the same period of time! Yet in what, if not in this marvellous train of coincidence, does the accidentally suggested opinion of the populace call upon us to believe?

"Before proceeding farther, let us consider the supposed scene of the assassination, in the thicket at the Barrière du Roule. This thicket, although dense, was in the close vicinity of a public road. Within were three or four large stones, forming a kind of seat with a back and footstool. On the upper stone was discovered a white petticoat; on the second, a silk scarf. A parasol, gloves, and a pocket-handkerchief, were also here found. The handkerchief bore the name, 'Marie Rogêt.' Fragments of dress were seen on the branches around. The earth was trampled, the bushes were broken, and there was every evidence of a violent struggle.

"Notwithstanding the acclamation with which the discovery of this thicket was received by the press, and the unanimity with which it was supposed to indicate the precise scene of the outrage, it must be admitted that there was some very good reason for doubt. That it was the scene, I may or I may not believe—but there was excellent reason for doubt.

Had the true scene been, as Le Commerciel suggested, in the neighborhood of the Rue Pavée St. Andrée, the perpetrators of the crime, supposing them still resident in Paris, would naturally have been stricken with terror at the public attention thus acutely directed into the proper channel; and, in certain classes of minds, there would have arisen, at once, a sense of the necessity of some exertion to redivert this attention. And thus, the thicket of the Barrière du Roule having been already suspected, the idea of placing the articles where they were found, might have been naturally entertained. There is no real evidence, although Le Soleil so supposes, that the articles discovered had been more than a very few days in the thicket; while there is much circumstantial proof that they could not have remained there, without attracting attention, during the

twenty days elapsing between the fatal
Sunday and the afternoon upon which
they were found by the boys. 'They were
all mildewed down hard,' says Le Soleil,
adopting the opinions of its
predecessors, 'with the action of the
rain, and stuck together from mildew.
The grass had grown around and over
some of them. The silk of the parasol
was strong, but the threads of it were
run together within. The upper part,
where it had been doubled and folded,
was all mildewed and rotten, and tore on
being opened.' In respect to the grass
having 'grown around and over some of
them,' it is obvious that the fact could
only have been ascertained from the
words, and thus from the recollections,
of two small boys; for these boys
removed the articles and took them
home before they had been seen by a
third party. But grass will grow,
especially in warm and damp weather,

(such as was that of the period of the murder,) as much as two or three inches in a single day. A parasol lying upon a newly turfed ground, might, in a single week, be entirely concealed from sight by the upspringing grass. And touching that mildew upon which the editor of Le Soleil so pertinaciously insists, that he employs the word no less than three times in the brief paragraph just quoted, is he really unaware of the nature of this mildew? Is he to be told that it is one of the many classes of fungus, of which the most ordinary feature is its upspringing and decadence within twenty-four hours?

"Thus we see, at a glance, that what has been most triumphantly adduced in support of the idea that the articles had been 'for at least three or four weeks' in the thicket, is most absurdly null as regards any evidence of that fact. On the other hand, it is exceedingly difficult to believe that these articles could have remained in the thicket specified, for a longer period than a single week—for a longer period than from one Sunday to the next. Those who know any thing of the vicinity of Paris, know the extreme difficulty of finding seclusion, unless at a great distance from its suburbs. Such a thing as an unexplored, or even an unfrequently visited recess, amid its woods or groves, is not for a moment to be imagined. Let any one who, being at heart a lover of nature, is yet chained by duty to the dust and heat of this great metropolis—let any such one attempt, even during the week-days, to slake his thirst for solitude amid the scenes of natural loveliness which immediately surround us. At every second step, he will find the growing charm dispelled by the voice and personal intrusion of some ruffian or party of carousing blackguards. He will seek privacy amid the densest foliage, all in vain. Here are the very nooks where the unwashed most abound—here are the temples most desecrate. With sickness of the heart the wanderer will flee back to the polluted Paris as to a less odious because less incongruous sink of pollution. But if the vicinity of the city is so beset during the working days of the week, how much more so on the Sabbath! It is now especially that, released from the claims of labor, or deprived of the customary opportunities of crime, the town blackguard seeks the precincts of the town, not through love of the rural, which in his heart he despises, but by way of escape from the restraints and conventionalities of society. He desires less the fresh air and the green trees, than the utter cense of the country. Here, at the road-side inn, or beneath the bliage of the woods, he indulges, unchecked by any eye except nose of his boon companions, in all the mad excess of a counterfeit hilarity—the joint offspring of liberty and of rum. I say nothing more than what must be obvious to every dispassionate observer, when I repeat that the circumstance of the articles in question having remained undiscovered, for a longer period than from one Sunday to another, in any thicket in the immediate neighborhood of Paris, is to be looked upon as little less than miraculous.

"But there are not wanting other grounds for the suspicion that the articles were placed in the thicket with the view of diverting attention from the real scene of the outrage. And, first, let me direct your notice to the date of the discovery of the articles. Collate this with the date of the fifth extract made by myself from the newspapers. You will find that the discovery followed, almost immediately, the urgent communications sent to the evening paper. These communications, although various, and apparently from various sources, tended all to the same point— viz., the directing of attention to a gang as the perpetrators of the outrage, and to the neighborhood of the Barrière du Roule as its scene. Now here, of course, the suspicion is not that, in consequence of these communications, or of the public attention by them directed, the articles were found by the boys; but the suspicion might and may well have been, that the articles were not before found by the boys, for the reason that the articles had not before been in the thicket; having been deposited there only at so late a period as at the date, or shortly prior to the date of the communications, by the guilty authors of these communications themselves.

"This thicket was a singular—an exceedingly singular one. It was unusually dense. Within its naturally walled enclosure were three extraordinary stones, forming a seat with a back and footstool. And this thicket, so full of a natural art, was in the immediate vicinity, within a few rods, of the dwelling of Madame Deluc, whose boys were in the habit of closely examining the shrubberies about them in search of the bark of the sassafras. Would it be a rash wager—a wager of one thousand to one—that a day never passed over the heads of these boys without finding at least one of them ensconced in the umbrageous hall, and enthroned upon its natural throne? Those who would hesitate at such a wager, have either never been boys themselves, or have forgotten the boyish nature. I repeat—it is exceedingly hard to comprehend how the articles could have remained in this thicket undiscovered, for a longer period than one or two days; and that thus there is good ground for suspicion, in spite of the dogmatic ignorance of Le Soleil, that they were, at a comparatively late date, deposited where found.

"But there are still other and stronger reasons for believing them so deposited, than any which I have as yet urged. And, now, let me beg your notice to the highly artificial arrangement of the articles. On the upper stone lay a white petticoat; on the second a silk scarf; scattered around, were a parasol, gloves, and a pocket-handkerchief bearing the name, 'Marie Rogêt.' Here is just such an arrangement as would naturally be made by a not-over-acute person wishing to dispose the articles naturally. But it is by no means a really natural arrangement. I should rather have looked to see the things all lying on the ground and trampled under foot. In the narrow limits of that bower, it would have been scarcely possible that the petticoat and scarf should have retained a position upon the stones, when subjected to the brushing to and fro of many struggling persons. 'There was evidence,' it is said, 'of a struggle; and the earth was trampled, the bushes were broken,'—but the petticoat and the scarf are found deposited as if upon shelves. 'The pieces of the frock torn out by the bushes were about three inches wide and six inches long. One part was the hem of the frock and it had been mended. They looked like strips torn off.' Here, inadvertently, Le Soleil has employed an exceedingly suspicious phrase. The pieces, as described, do indeed 'look like strips torn off;' but purposely and by hand. It is one of the rarest of accidents that a piece is 'torn off,' from any garment such as is now in question, by the agency of a thorn. From the very nature of such fabrics, a thorn or nail becoming entangled in them, tears them rectangularly—divides them into two longitudinal rents, at right angles with each other, and meeting at an apex where the thorn enters—but it is scarcely possible to conceive the piece 'torn off.' I never so knew it, nor did you. To tear a piece off from such fabric, two distinct forces, in different directions, will be, in almost every case, required. If there be two edges to the fabric—if, for example, it be a pocket-handkerchief, and it is desired to tear from it a slip, then, and then only, will the one force serve the purpose. But in the present case the question is of a dress, presenting but one edge. To tear a piece from the interior, where no edge is presented, could only be effected by a miracle through the agency of thorns, and no one thorn could accomplish it. But, even where an edge is presented, two thorns will be necessary, operating, the one in two distinct directions, and the other in one. And this in the supposition that the edge is unhemmed. If hemmed, the matter is nearly out of the question. We thus see the numerous and great obstacles in the way of pieces being 'torn off' through the simple agency of 'thorn;' yet we are required to believe not only that one piece but that many have been so torn. 'And one part,' too, 'was the hem of the frock!' Another piece was 'part of the skirt, not the hem, '—that is to say, was torn completely out, through the agency of thorns, from the unedged interior of the dress! These, I say, are things which one may well be pardoned for disbelieving; yet, taken collectedly, they form, perhaps, less of reasonable ground for suspicion, than the one startling circumstance of the articles' having been left in this thicket at all, by any murderers who had enough precaution to think of removing the corpse. You will not have apprehended me rightly, however, if you suppose it my design to deny this thicket as the scene of the outrage. There might have been a wrong here, or, more possibly, an accident at Madame Deluc's. But, in fact, this is a point of minor importance. We are not engaged in an attempt to discover the scene, but to produce the perpetrators of the murder. What I have adduced, notwithstanding the minuteness with which I have adduced it, has been with the view, first, to show the folly of the positive and headlong assertions of Le Soleil, but secondly and chiefly, to bring you, by the most natural route, to a further contemplation of the doubt whether this assassination has, or has not been, the work of a gang.

"We will resume this question by mere allusion to the revolting details of the surgeon examined at the inquest. It is only necessary to say that his published inferences, in regard to the number of the ruffians, have been properly ridiculed as unjust and totally baseless, by all the reputable anatomists of Paris. Not that the matter might not have been as inferred, but that there was no ground for the inference:—was there not much for another?

"Let us reflect now upon 'the traces of a struggle;' and let me ask what these traces have been supposed to demonstrate. A gang. But do they not rather demonstrate the absence of a gang? What struggle could have taken place—what struggle so violent and so enduring as to have left its 'traces' in all directions— between a weak and defenseless girl and the gang of ruffians imagined? The silent grasp of a few rough arms and all would have been over. The victim must have been absolutely passive at their will. You will here bear in mind that the arguments urged against the thicket as the scene, are applicable, in chief part, only against it as the scene of an outrage committed by more than a single individual. If we imagine but one violator, we can conceive, and thus only conceive, the struggle of so violent and so obstinate a nature as to have left the 'traces' apparent.

"And again. I have already mentioned the suspicion to be excited by the fact that the articles in question were suffered to remain at all in the thicket where discovered. It seems almost impossible that these evidences of guilt should have been accidentally left where found. There was sufficient presence of

mind (it is supposed) to remove the
corpse; and yet a more positive evidence
than the corpse itself (whose features
might have been quickly obliterated by
decay,) is allowed to lie conspicuously in
the scene of the outrage—I allude to the
handkerchief with the name of the
deceased. If this was accident, it was not
the accident of a gang. We can imagine it
only the accident of an individual. Let us
see. An individual has committed the
murder. He is alone with the ghost of
the departed. He is appalled by what lies
motionless before him. The fury of his
passion is over, and there is abundant
room in his heart for the natural awe of
the deed. His is none of that confidence
which the presence of numbers
inevitably inspires. He is alone with the
dead. He trembles and is bewildered.
Yet there is a necessity for disposing of
the corpse. He bears it to the river, but
leaves behind him the other evidences of

guilt; for it is difficult, if not impossible
to carry all the burthen at once, and it
will be easy to return for what is left. But
in his toilsome journey to the water his
fears redouble within him. The sounds
of life encompass his path. A dozen
times he hears or fancies the step of an
observer. Even the very lights from the
city bewilder him. Yet, in time, and by
long and frequent pauses of deep agony,
he reaches the river's brink, and
disposes of his ghastly charge—perhaps
through the medium of a boat. But now
what treasure does the world hold—
what threat of vengeance could it hold
out—which would have power to urge
the return of that lonely murderer over
that toilsome and perilous path, to the
thicket and its blood-chilling
recollections? He returns not, let the
consequences be what they may. He
could not return if he would. His sole
thought is immediate escape. He turns

his back forever upon those dreadful shrubberies, and flees as from the wrath to come.

"But how with a gang? Their number would have inspired them with confidence; if, indeed, confidence is ever wanting in the breast of the arrant blackguard; and of arrant blackguards alone are the supposed gangs ever constituted. Their number, I say, would have prevented the bewildering and unreasoning terror which I have imagined to paralyze the single man. Could we suppose an oversight in one, or two, or three, this oversight would have been remedied by a fourth. They would have left nothing behind them; for their number would have enabled them to carry all at once. There would have been no need of return.

"Consider now the circumstance that, in the outer garment of the corpse when found, 'a slip, about a foot wide, had been torn upward from the bottom hem to the waist, wound three times round the waist, and secured by a sort of hitch in the back.' This was done with the obvious design of affording a handle by which to carry the body. But would any number of men have dreamed of resorting to such an expedient? To three or four, the limbs of the corpse would have afforded not only a sufficient, but the best possible hold. The device is that of a single individual; and this brings us to the fact that 'between the thicket and the river, the rails of the fences were found taken down, and the ground bore evident traces of some heavy burden having been dragged along it!' But would a number of men have put themselves to the superfluous trouble of taking down a fence, for the purpose of dragging through it a corpse which they might have lifted over any fence in an instant? Would a number of men have so dragged a corpse at all as to have left evident traces of the dragging?

"And here we must refer to an observation of Le Commerciel; an observation upon which I have already, in some measure, commented. 'A piece,' says this journal, 'of one of the unfortunate girl's petticoats was torn out and tied under her chin, and around the back of her head, probably to prevent screams. This was done by fellows who had no pocket-handkerchiefs.'

"I have before suggested that a genuine blackguard is never without a pocket-handkerchief. But it is not to this fact that I now especially advert. That it was not through want of a handkerchief for the purpose imagined by Le

Commerciel, that this bandage was employed, is rendered apparent by the handkerchief left in the thicket; and that the object was not 'to prevent screams' appears, also, from the bandage having been employed in preference to what would so much better have answered the purpose. But the language of the evidence speaks of the strip in question as 'found around the neck, fitting loosely, and secured with a hard knot.' These words are sufficiently vague, but differ materially from those of Le Commerciel. The slip was eighteen inches wide, and therefore, although of muslin, would form a strong band when folded or rumpled longitudinally. And thus rumpled it was discovered. My inference is this. The solitary murderer, having borne the corpse, for some distance, (whether from the thicket or elsewhere) by means of the bandage hitched around its middle, found the weight, in this mode of procedure, too much for his strength. He resolved to drag the burthen—the evidence goes to show that it was dragged. With this object in view, it became necessary to attach something like a rope to one of the extremities. It could be best attached about the neck, where the head would prevent its slipping off. And, now, the murderer bethought him, unquestionably, of the bandage about the loins. He would have used this, but for its volution about the corpse, the hitch which embarrassed it, and the reflection that it had not been 'torn off' from the garment. It was easier to tear a new slip from the petticoat. He tore it, made it fast about the neck, and so dragged his victim to the brink of the river. That this 'bandage,' only attainable with trouble and delay, and but imperfectly answering its purpose—that this bandage was employed at all, demonstrates that the necessity for its employment sprang from circumstances arising at a period when the handkerchief was no longer attainable—that is to say, arising, as we have imagined, after quitting the thicket, (if the thicket it was), and on the road between the thicket and the river.

"But the evidence, you will say, of Madame Deluc, (!) points especially to the presence of a gang, in the vicinity of the thicket, at or about the epoch of the murder. This I grant. I doubt if there were not a dozen gangs, such as described by Madame Deluc, in and about the vicinity of the Barrière du Roule at or about the period of this tragedy. But the gang which has drawn upon itself the pointed animadversion, although the somewhat tardy and very suspicious evidence of Madame Deluc, is the only gang which is represented by that honest and scrupulous old lady as having eaten her cakes and swallowed her brandy, without putting themselves to the trouble of making her payment. Et hinc illoe iroe?

"But what is the precise evidence of Madame Deluc? 'A gang of miscreants made their appearance, behaved boisterously, ate and drank without making payment, followed in the route of the young man and girl, returned to the inn about dusk, and recrossed the river as if in great haste.'

"Now this 'great haste' very possibly seemed greater haste in the eyes of Madame Deluc, since she dwelt lingeringly and lamentingly upon her violated cakes and ale—cakes and ale for which she might still have entertained a faint hope of compensation. Why, otherwise, since it was about dusk, should she make a point of the haste? It is no cause for wonder, surely, that even a gang of blackguards should make haste to get home, when a wide river is to be crossed in small boats, when storm impends, and when night approaches .

"I say approaches; for the night had not yet arrived. It was only about dusk that the indecent haste of these 'miscreants' offended the sober eyes of Madame Deluc. But we are told that it was upon this very evening that Madame Deluc, as well as her eldest son, 'heard the screams of a female in the vicinity of the inn.' And in what words does Madame Deluc designate the period of the evening at which these screams were heard? 'It was soon after dark,' she says. But 'soon after dark,' is, at least, dark; and ' about dusk' is as certainly daylight. Thus it is abundantly clear that the gang quitted the Barrière du Roule prior to

the screams overheard (?) by Madame
Deluc. And although, in all the many
reports of the evidence, the relative
expressions in question are distinctly
and invariably employed just as I have
employed them in this conversation with
yourself, no notice whatever of the gross
discrepancy has, as yet, been taken by
any of the public journals, or by any of
the Myrmidons of police.

"I shall add but one to the arguments
against a gang; but this one has, to my
own understanding at least, a weight
altogether irresistible. Under the
circumstances of large reward offered,
and full pardon to any King's evidence, it
is not to be imagined, for a moment, that
some member of a gang of low ruffians,
or of any body of men, would not long
ago have betrayed his accomplices. Each
one of a gang so placed, is not so much
greedy of reward, or anxious for escape,

as fearful of betrayal. He betrays eagerly and early that he may not himself be betrayed. That the secret has not been divulged, is the very best of proof that it is, in fact, a secret. The horrors of this dark deed are known only to one, or two, living human beings, and to God.

"Let us sum up now the meagre yet certain fruits of our long analysis. We have attained the idea either of a fatal accident under the roof of Madame Deluc, or of a murder perpetrated, in the thicket at the Barrière du Roule, by a lover, or at least by an intimate and secret associate of the deceased. This associate is of swarthy complexion. This complexion, the 'hitch' in the bandage, and the 'sailor's knot,' with which the bonnet-ribbon is tied, point to a seaman. His companionship with the deceased, a gay, but not an abject young girl, designates him as above the grade of the common sailor. Here the well written and urgent communications to the journals are much in the way of corroboration. The circumstance of the first elopement, as mentioned by Le Mercurie, tends to blend the idea of this seaman with that of the 'naval officer' who is first known to have led the unfortunate into crime.

"And here, most fitly, comes the consideration of the continued absence of him of the dark complexion. Let me pause to observe that the complexion of this man is dark and swarthy; it was no common swarthiness which constituted the sole point of remembrance, both as regards Valence and Madame Deluc. But why is this man absent? Was he murdered by the gang? If so, why are there only traces of the assassinated girl? The scene of the two outrages will naturally be supposed identical. And where is his corpse? The assassins would most probably have disposed of both in the same way. But it may be said that this man lives, and is deterred from making himself known, through dread of being charged with the murder. This consideration might be supposed to operate upon him now—at this late period—since it has been given in evidence that he was seen with Marie—but it would have had no force at the period of the deed. The first impulse of an innocent man would have been to announce the outrage, and to aid in identifying the ruffians. This, policy would have suggested. He had been seen with the girl. He had crossed the river with her in an open ferry-boat. The denouncing of the assassins would have appeared, even to an idiot, the surest and sole means of relieving himself from suspicion. We cannot suppose him, on the night of the fatal Sunday, both innocent himself and incognizant of an outrage committed. Yet only under such circumstances is it possible to imagine that he would have failed, if alive, in the denouncement of the assassins.

"And what means are ours, of attaining the truth? We shall find these means multiplying and gathering distinctness as we proceed. Let us sift to the bottom this affair of the first elope ment. Let us know the full history of 'the officer,' with his present circumstances, and his whereabouts at the precise period of the murder. Let us carefully compare with each other the various communications sent to the evening paper, in which the object was to inculpate a gang. This done, let us compare these communications, both as regards style and MS., with those sent to the morning paper, at a previous period, and insisting so vehemently upon the guilt of

Mennais. And, all this done, let us again compare these various communications with the known MSS. of the officer. Let us endeavor to ascertain, by repeated questionings of Madame Deluc and her boys, as well as of the omnibus-driver, Valence, something more of the personal appearance and bearing of the 'man of dark complexion.' Queries, skilfully directed, will not fail to elicit, from some of these parties, information on this particular point (or upon others)—information which the parties themselves may not even be aware of possessing. And let us now trace the boat picked up by the bargeman on the morning of Monday the twenty-third of June, and which was removed from the barge-office, without the cognizance of the officer in attendance, and without the rudder, at some period prior to the discovery of the corpse. With a proper caution and perseverance we shall

infallibly trace this boat; for not only can
the bargeman who picked it up identify
it, but the rudder is at hand. The rudder
of a sail-boat would not have been
abandoned, without inquiry, by one
altogether at ease in heart. And here let
me pause to insinuate a question. There
was no advertisement of the picking up
of this boat. It was silently taken to the
barge-office, and as silently removed.
But its owner or employer—how
happened he, at so early a period as
Tuesday morning, to be informed,
without the agency of advertisement, of
the locality of the boat taken up on
Monday, unless we imagine some
connexion with the navy—some
personal permanent connexion leading
to cognizance of its minute interests—its
petty local news?

"In speaking of the lonely assassin
dragging his burden to the shore, I have

already suggested the probability of his availing himself of a boat. Now we are to understand that Marie Rogêt was precipitated from a boat. This would naturally have been the case. The corpse could not have been trusted to the shallow waters of the shore. The peculiar marks on the back and shoulders of the victim tell of the bottom ribs of a boat. That the body was found without weight is also corroborative of the idea. If thrown from the shore a weight would have been attached. We can only account for its absence by supposing the murderer to have neglected the precaution of supplying himself with it before pushing off. In the act of consigning the corpse to the water, he would unquestionably have noticed his oversight; but then no remedy would have been at hand. Any risk would have been preferred to a return to that accursed shore. Having rid himself of his ghastly charge, the murderer would have hastened to the city. There, at some obscure wharf, he would have leaped on land. But the boat—would he have secured it? He would have been in too great haste for such things as securing a boat. Moreover, in fastening it to the wharf, he would have felt as if securing evidence against himself. His natural thought would have been to cast from him, as far as possible, all that had held connection with his crime. He would not only have fled from the wharf, but he would not have permitted the boat to remain. Assuredly he would have cast it adrift. Let us pursue our fancies.—In the morning, the wretch is stricken with unutterable horror at finding that the boat has been picked up and detained at a locality which he is in the daily habit of frequenting— at a locality, perhaps, which his duty compels him to frequent. The next night, without daring to ask for the rudder, he removes it. Now where is that rudderless boat? Let it be one of our first purposes to discover. With the first glimpse we obtain of it, the dawn of our success shall begin. This boat shall guide us, with a rapidity which will surprise even ourselves, to him who employed it in the midnight of the fatal Sabbath. Corroboration will rise upon corroboration, and the murderer will be traced."

It will be understood that I speak of coincidences and no more . What I have said above upon this topic must suffice. In my own heart there dwells no faith in præter-nature. That Nature and its God are two, no man who thinks, will deny. That the latter, creating the former, can, at will, control or modify it, is also unquestionable. I say "at will;" for the question is of will, and not, as the insanity of logic has assumed, of power.

It is not that the Deity cannot modify his laws, but that we insult him in imagining a possible necessity for modification. In their origin these laws were fashioned to embrace all contingencies which could lie in the Future. With God all is Now.

I repeat, then, that I speak of these things only as of coincidences. And farther: in what I relate it will be seen that between the fate of the unhappy Mary Cecilia Rogers, so far as that fate is known, and the fate of one Marie Rogêt up to a certain epoch in her history, there has existed a parallel in the contemplation of whose wonderful exactitude the reason becomes embarrassed. I say all this will be seen. But let it not for a moment be supposed that, in proceeding with the sad narrative of Marie from the epoch just mentioned, and in tracing to its dénouement the mystery which enshrouded her, it is my covert design to hint at an extension of the parallel, or even to suggest that the measures adopted in Paris for the discovery of the assassin of a grisette, or measures founded in any similar ratiocination, would produce any similar result.

For, in respect to the latter branch of the supposition, it should be considered that the most trifling variation in the facts of the two cases might give rise to the most important miscalculations, by diverting thoroughly the two courses of events; very much as, in arithmetic, an error which, in its own individuality, may be inappreciable, produces, at length, by dint of multiplication at all points of the process, a result enormously at variance with truth. And, in regard to the former branch, we must not fail to hold in view that the very Calculus of Probabilities to

which I have referred, forbids all idea of
the extension of the parallel:—forbids it
with a positiveness strong and decided
just in proportion as this parallel has
already been long-drawn and exact. This
is one of those anomalous propositions
which, seemingly appealing to thought
altogether apart from the mathematical,
is yet one which only the mathematician
can fully entertain. Nothing, for
example, is more difficult than to
convince the merely general reader that
the fact of sixes having been thrown
twice in succession by a player at dice, is
sufficient cause for betting the largest
odds that sixes will not be thrown in the
third attempt. A suggestion to this effect
is usually rejected by the intellect at
once. It does not appear that the two
throws which have been completed, and
which lie now absolutely in the Past, can
have influence upon the throw which
exists only in the Future. The chance for

throwing sixes seems to be precisely as it was at any ordinary time— that is to say, subject only to the influence of the various other throws which may be made by the dice. And this is a reflection which appears so exceedingly obvious that attempts to controvert it are received more frequently with a derisive smile than with anything like respectful attention. The error here involved—a gross error redolent of mischief—I cannot pretend to expose within the limits assigned me at present; and with the philosophical it needs no exposure. It may be sufficient here to say that it forms one of an infinite series of mistakes which arise in the path or Reason through her propensity for seeking truth in detail.